T0381210

The Secret Revealed

Tony DeBerardinis

Illustrated by: Laura Walker

AuthorHouse™
1663 Liberty Drive
Bloomington, IN 47403
www.authorhouse.com
Phone: 1 (800) 839-8640

Published by AuthorHouse: 08/06/2015

ISBN: 978-1-5049-2527-3 (sc)
ISBN: 978-1-5049-2528-0 (e)

DEDICATION

To all my grandchildren. I hope these stories have given you a desire to use your imagination. You are all very special and precious to me.

The Secret Revealed

Chapter 1

Fifteen years have passed since the cave-in and rescue of Curtis. The gravity machine was safe, but more people have gone into the tunnel to explore. Thankfully, no one has dug behind the wall of rubble to find the cave…or so they thought. One of the volunteers who helped with the rescue of Curtis has found the cave and is making plans for something devious.

Meanwhile, Curtis, and his father, Lukas, who adopted him, were at home getting ready for Curtis' graduation from college.

"Dad!" Curtis said, "Stop squirming and let me finish tying your tie."

Lukas tilted his head back and said, "Sorry son. I'm just so excited!"

"The way you're acting, you would think it was you, who was graduating." replied Curtis with a laugh.

"Valedictorian! Giving the big speech in front of all those people," Lukas said with a big smile. "I don't know if I could do that. Have all those people looking at me while I'm talking. I'd probably sound like an idiot."

"Are you trying to make me nervous? Because you're doing a good job!"

Curtis straightened his father's collar and adjusted his tie. Lukas placed his hands on Curtis' shoulders and looked him in the eyes and said,

"I'm sorry son. I know you'll do just fine. Shall we go?"

Curtis and Lukas made their way to the University. It seemed everybody from their home town was there to see Curtis graduate. Lukas gave Curtis one last hug before letting him go to his classmates.

"Go get 'em tiger!" his grandfather hollered out as Curtis ran through the crowd, dodging people left and right.

As everyone was getting to their seats, the University Director approached the microphone.

"Would you please stand for the playing of the National Anthem and prayer."

After the prayer, the president of the university got up and thanked everyone for attending this year's graduation. He introduced his staff and then delivered a speech to the graduates about the importance of accomplishing their dreams.

"...and now for my favorite part of the ceremony. It is my pleasure to introduce to you this year's Valedictorian. Please give a warm welcome to Curtis…"

The president could not be heard because of the roar of the crowd cheering and applauding. Curtis rose up and made his way to the stage. He shook the president's hand and turned to face the audience. They were still applauding him. He raised one hand up and they quieted down. Then he looked at his classmates and said with a big smile,

"The sooner I finish, the sooner we can get our diplomas and get out of here!"

The students burst into laughter and cheers. After it had gotten silent again, Curtis started his speech.

"It is a great honor to be up here today. I'm not sure if what I'm about to do is in good standing with the school or not."

A student yelled out. "It's your stage Curtis, go for it!"

"There is another student that deserves to be up here with me, my friend, Mariska Brookes! Mariska, come up here!"

The class cheered again as Curtis met Mariska at the stage steps. They stood together. Then Curtis, after the applauses stopped, started his speech. He thanked all his friends and teachers and talked about his experience throughout school. He was about finished and said,

"In conclusion, I have one other person I would like to mention. I am one of the lucky few who have been given a chance to make something of myself. I was raised in an orphanage until my father…Dad…stand up. Until my father adopted me and started me on a path that would forever change my life. I won't go through all the details of my life, but, I just wanted to say in front of everyone here, Dad, I owe you so much. You saved my life twice. The first time when I was trapped in the cave and the second time when you adopted me as your son. You've given me a loving home, full of family and friends. Well, today it's my turn to give you something back. My diploma! Thanks Dad!"

Everyone cheered and graduation hats flew in the air.

Lukas looked at Curtis with tears in his eyes and gave him a thumbs up.

Chapter 2

After the graduation was over, Curtis and his friends went to their party. Lukas and his dad headed for home.

"I'm so proud of him Dad!" he said.

"I should say so." Pete replied. "And how about that job offer he got? Makes me wish I was his age again."

"I think we all wish that at some point. Especially as we get older."

"That's the truth!" his father said as they both started to laugh.

"Pull into the diner there and I'll buy us some coffee and pie."

Lukas parked the truck and they went inside. They sat in the diner enjoying their snack and talking about old times. A few minutes passed by and Mayor Wilson walked in. They invited her to their table and to have a slice of pie and coffee.

"That was some graduation." She said as she sat down. "You must be very proud of Curtis?"

Lukas helped her with her chair and said, "Yes, yes I am," He thought a moment and continued speaking. "Funny how things work out the way they do. I remember when I first met Jeremy. I sure was a brat!" he chuckled. "Yet, he gave me a second chance. Maybe that's why I adopted Curtis. Someone needed to give him a second chance and I had the ability to do that."

"That's how things work son," Pete said, "When people do good things to you, you should do the same to others. And if they do you wrong, let it go, and do good anyways. It's a hidden blessing."

After the waitress brought the Mayor her pie and coffee, and refilled the other cups, she asked if they needed anything else. No one did.

Then the Mayor said, "I have a concern I need to speak to you both about. As you know, this town is growing rapidly. We know that the tunnel is going to be explored more and more. The 'Danger Keep Out' sign only does so much. Lukas, I know removing and replacing those rocks to get to the gravity machine is getting very tiresome for you."

Lukas replied, "Curtis is the one taking care of the machine most of the time now. I do admit, moving all those rocks is getting harder. Most of all it's just not safe."

"She's right Luke." His father said. "Someone is bound to go in and work their way into the cave. We could end up with a major problem if someone gets in there and breaks something."

"Let's give it some thought." replied Lukas. "Surely we can come up with some ideas to solve this problem. I know people go in there. I've seen the remains of camp fires and trash. Let's meet back here in a couple of days with some ideas. Until then, I will go to the tunnel more often just to make sure no one is getting into the cave."

Chapter 3

Meanwhile, in a hotel room in town, Mr. Williams, the man who led the team in the rescue of Curtis, years ago, was plotting a bank robbery. He and two other men, Joe and Rocco, were sitting at a table discussing the plot.

"I've been waiting a long time for this!" Mr. Williams said angrily, as he paced the floor. "I helped them save that kid and all I got was a lousy dinner! Our plans have changed boys. I have discovered something that is going to make this job very easy."

"What is that Mr. Williams?" asked Joe.

"While we were getting that kid out of the tunnel, they seem to want to keep everyone away from behind the wall of rubble. I didn't pay it no mind for a long time." He continued, "I went back there just the other day and found something that is absolutely amazing. They are hiding a machine. A machine that controls the gravity in this town."

"Hey!" Rocco said, "That could be really handy."

"Yes!" Mr. Williams said, with his eyes wide open. "I think we could use that machine to our advantage. I think if we time things just right, we can rob the town bank and all the stores and make a clean get away!"

"Well what are we waiting for?" replied Joe. "Let's start the new plans."

The men got together at the table. They had maps and charts of the town spread out in front of them and started to plan their devious plot.

Chapter 4

The next day, Curtis went to meet Dr. Barnsdale about getting some money from the university for an experiment he and Mariska were developing.

"Hi Dr. Barnsdale," Curtis said as he shook his hand. "I'm Curtis, I spoke with you on the phone the other day about a grant."

"Yes, Curtis. How are you? Come in and sit down," replied Dr. Barnsdale, "I'm very interested in this whole idea of yours."

"I designed a special door. This door will not have a common key, nor will it have a combination. So it will be impossible for anyone to open it without the proper mechanism."

"Sounds wonderful! If it works, big companies maybe be interested in it. That could boost, not only the University's name, but yours as well. What can you tell me about this door of yours?"

Curtis stood up with enthusiasm and started to tell him. "Well for starters, I'm designing a new metal. A friend of mine is working on a state of the art locking mechanism. We think it is very possible to make a door that is very light-weight, very thin, yet stronger than any other metal door designed. All with a locking device that will be absolutely impenetrable."

"Sounds very promising," the doctor said, as he stood up and walked over to Curtis. "If your friend is here now, give him a call and let's get this project started."

Curtis smiled and said, "Yes…'She' is here. Her name is Mariska Brookes. She's in the lab right now. Can we meet here in your office at 2:30 this afternoon?"

Dr. Barnsdale shook his hand and said, "That will be just fine. I will see you both this afternoon."

When Curtis got back home late that afternoon, he called the Mayor.

"Hello, Mayor Wilson's office. How may I help you?" Asked the secretary.

"This is Curtis. The Mayor is expecting my call."

"I'll put you through to her office. Hold please."

"This is Mayor Wilson. Can I help you?"

"Hi Mayor, this is Curtis."

"Hello Curtis! It's so good to hear from you. Have you heard anything about the grant you've been needing?"

"As a matter of fact I have. I have good news. Dr. Barnsdale has agreed to give us a grant to design a new metal and a new door. The best part is that he is going to allow us to use the cave and tunnel to test it on."

"That's wonderful!" The Mayor said with excitement. "How long do you think it will be before you get started?"

"Hopefully within the next couple of days. I've already got the special metal developed. And Mariska has the door designed and the mechanisms to open the door ready. We just needed the money to help pay for a bigger project. I think you're going to really like what we have in store," Curtis said with enthusiasm. "You will need three people you can trust to open this door. I will fill you in on the details when we get closer to installing the door. Just don't tell them what we are doing."

"I'll start screening for those people first thing in the morning. If you need anything, let me know. Thank you Curtis. Good bye."

Chapter 5

The next morning, Mayor Wilson started to make some phone calls. She set up interviews for the afternoon to choose the three people who she thought she could trust the most.

"Hello Mr. Williams? Mayor Wilson here. Listen, I've decided I would like you to be part of a special top secret project we talked about earlier today. Are you still interested?"

"Count me in Mayor. When do we start?"

"In a couple of days. I'll be in touch. Good bye."

Then the Mayor called the other two people she chose and they also agreed to be part of the secret project.

A couple days later, Curtis and Mariska were in the cave going over some last details.

"Hi Mariska. Are you ready to install the door?"

"Yes. I've tested it at the lab to make sure it's in good working order. It will take a short time to put it up. Then it's up to you to do your thing. Tell me again. How does this secret metal work?"

"Well, to put it simply, it's like taking a garden hose and spraying a wall or door with water. Only I'm spraying it with a liquid metal that hardens on contact with any surface within just a few minutes. I'm going to spray the entire cave and tunnel top to bottom. This will stop someone from digging into the tunnel or cave and prevent any cave-ins."

"That's great! I have a surprise for you I think you're going to like. I'll show you after the door is finished." Mariska smiled.

The next day, Curtis and Mariska met with Mayor Wilson.

"Hi Mayor. Did you choose the three people you feel you could trust with the secret door?" asked Curtis.

"Yes, I did." She replied. "My sister Pam, Mr. Williams, and I thought Mr. White, the bank manager, would be a good choice."

"Okay. Before we start, we need to discuss a few things. The people you have chosen are not to know about each other. If one of them leave's town, they must bring their mechanism, well, it's actually a disc for opening the door. They must bring that to you. They are not to go into the cave without permission. Finally, these people must be sworn to secrecy. I think that's all." Curtis turned to Mariska and asked her, "Can you think of anything else?"

"Nope," she replied, "I think that covers it."

Later that day, the Mayor had the three people she had chosen to come to her office at separate times. First her sister, then Mr. White and finally, Mr. Williams showed up for the briefing.

"Hello, Mr. Williams, come in." The Mayor shook his hand as he came to the chair in front of her desk and sat down. She explained all the details to him and then she handed him a silver disc.

"Is this the key?" He asked. "I've never seen anything like it before."

"It's magnetic." the Mayor explained. "Just place it above the door handle, wait one minute, and the door will automatically open."

"That's it!?" He said in amazement.

"That's it. It's that simple. Don't forget the rules. I certainly appreciate you taking on this responsibility. Thank you Mr. Williams. If you have any questions, feel free to stop by."

"Thank you Mayor for trusting me. You have a wonderful day, goodbye."

Mr. Williams left the office with a big smile on his face. He thought to himself, 'This is going to be easier than I could have hoped for!'

Chapter 6

After Mr. Williams left the office he went straight to see his two buddies.

"Guess what boys?" He asked.

"What?" They said together.

"I have good news and bad news."

"What's the bad news," asked Rocco "I like to hear the bad news first. That way, maybe the good news will make me feel better."

"Well…the bad news is…" Mr. Williams said with his head hung low. "…the bad is, they have built a door that is impossible to break into."

"What!?" cried out Joe. "That just ruined all our plans! Now what do we do?"

"There's nothing we can do except rob the bank the old fashion way." said Rocco as he threw his hands up in the air.

"Hold on a minute now," said Mr. Williams. "I haven't told you the good news." He smiled as he held up a silver disc. "I have the key boys!
Let's make this Friday our big day!"

The three of them spent the next couple of days making their plans, gathering equipment and supplies, to rob the bank while the gravity machine was off.

Chapter 7

It was Friday morning, Curtis was at the lab with Mariska.

"You did a really good job on that door Mariska. And those added security measures will be a great selling point for any businesses interested in buying our product."

Mariska smiled and said, "Thank you Curtis. It's because of you that I have the opportunity to try my door out in the first place. I just hope it works well enough in this trial phase. Maybe…"

Just then the phone rang.

"Hello. Tech Lab 1. Mariska speaking. Oh, hold on Mayor, I'll put you on speaker phone." Mariska pressed the speaker button and said, "Okay Mayor, we can both hear you."

"Hey guys. I know we are going to experience some glitches with our new door…" she paused a moment.

"What is it Mayor?" asked Curtis.

"Well…that emergency light you installed in my office is flashing."

"It's probably nothing," replied Mariska. "But let's use this opportunity to practice this as a real problem. Mayor, you call the police and tell them we are treating this as if it were a real emergency. Curtis and I will call Lukas, and we will meet you at the tunnel entrance."

Chapter 8

Curtis, Mariska and Lukas, arrived at the tunnel and was surprised at what they seen.

"It worked!" proclaimed Mariska as she jumped up and down, clapping her hands.

"What's this?" asked Lukas. As he stared with astonishment at the three men behind bars in the tunnel.

"Oh no, Mr. Williams!" Curtis said.

Just then the Mayor and the Chief of Police drove up and could not believe what they saw.

"Get me out of here!" yelled Mr. Williams.

"Well, well, well," said the Mayor. "What a surprise! I thought you were an honest man, but I see by the look of things that, I was very wrong."

The police chief spoke up, "I've seen tools like this before, they're used to break into a bank vault. But I don't know what these are?" Pointing at some big rubber cups.

"I get it now." Lukas said. "Those are suction cups to wear on their feet. You were going to turn off the gravity machine. Then you were going to use the suction cups so that you wouldn't float off the ground like everyone else and rob the town bank."

"Aren't you the smart one!?" Mr. Williams said angrily. "The plan was perfect! But thanks to these two kids, the disc to open this door was faulty."

The Mayor, Curtis and Mariska started laughing. No one else knew why they were laughing so much. They didn't understand what was so funny.

Mariska spoke up and explained. "The door worked exactly the way it was designed to. We built in a security system to keep people like you…" she said as she pointed to the three men. "… from unauthorized entry. You were told not to enter this area without permission, but you chose to ignore the rules."

Mr. Williams' two buddies looked at him and said, "Way to go boss! You said you had everything under control!"

"It was!" yelled Mr. Williams, as he stuck his hand out between the bars with the disc clutched in his fist, shaking it. "I was told this disc would open the door, not trap us!"

Curtis quickly grabbed the disc from his hand. "I'll take that! This disc will open the door…sort of. But, like Mariska said, you didn't follow the rules."

After opening the bars, the police hand cuffed the three men and took them to jail. Mariska and Curtis reset the security system. After everything was back in order, they all went back to town. The two of them explained how the door and the security system really worked.

Chapter 9

When they got back to town, they all went to the coffee shop. Everyone had pie and listened to Lukas tell his story about how he had met Jeremy, and all the adventures he had. He saved the best for last. The one where he forgot to turn the key and the gravity stopped holding everything on the ground. And, how he fixed the problem. After a while, the conversation turned back to the events of the day.

"I feel so much better knowing we have a security system for the gravity machine." said Mayor Wilson.

"It's going to make my job a lot easier." Curtis said, as he looked at Mariska and winked his eye.

"So…" Lukas asked with curiosity. "…all three keys, or disc's, had to be used at the same time, in order for the door to open without setting off the security alarm?"

Mayor Wilson said, "That's right. If only one or two of the disc's are used, well, as you just saw, it sets off the security system and automatically traps the 'would be' intruders."

Mariska added. "Curtis is the only person that has a single disc that will open the door without tripping the alarm."

"That's right," Curtis said. "One day, when I get too old to take care of the gravity machine, I will pass it on to someone I know to be trustworthy."

"I wish Jeremy were here to see all that has taken place," Lukas said. "He would be so proud of both of you."

The gravity machine was finally safe. Because of what happened to Mr. Williams, and his two buddies, word got around about the security door. There were no more attempts made to break into the cave. Curtis continued to go there from time-to-time to make sure everything worked as it should. Lukas would go with him on occasion, just to remember how he got started with this adventure.

Curtis and Mariska were married several years later and had a baby girl named, Sabrina. When she was old enough, she began to take care of the gravity machine. And so it was passed down from generation to generation. The gravity machine was always cared for and the town never lost its gravity again.

About the Author

Tony has a unique way of making a child read into his book and giving them the feeling that they are right there in the action. His vivid imagination is seen with every turn of the page.

Printed in the United States
By Bookmasters